Vera Runs Away

Vera Rosenberry

Henry Holt and Company

New York

Henry Holt and Company, LLC
Publishers since 1866
115 West 18th Street, New York, New York 10011

Henry Holt is a registered trademark of Henry Holt and Company, LLC
Copyright © 2000 by Vera Rosenberry. All rights reserved.
Published in Canada by Fitzhenry & Whiteside Ltd., 195 Allstate Parkway, Markham, Ontario L3R 4T8.

Library of Congress Cataloging-in-Publication Data
Rosenberry, Vera. Vera runs away / Vera Rosenberry.
Summary: When her family seems to be too busy to appreciate her
good report card, first-grader Vera decides to find somewhere else to live.
[1. Family life—Fiction. 2. Runaways—Fiction.] I. Title.
PZ7.R719155Vd 2000 [E]—dc21 99-33611

ISBN 0-8050-6267-X / First Edition—2000 / Designed by Donna Mark
Printed in the United States of America on acid-free paper. ∞

1 3 5 7 9 10 8 6 4 2

The artist used gouache on Lanaquarelle paper to create the illustrations for this book.

To Christy O.,
for all her support and encouragement

It was a balmy spring afternoon, full of flowery smells.
Vera skipped along on her way home from school.

Norman caught up with her.

"Show me your report card, Vera, and I'll show you mine."

Vera pulled her report card out of her book bag.

"Wow!" Norman said. "You got A's in everything!

"If I had your report card, my mother would make pizza for dinner and chocolate cake for dessert. Maybe she would even take me to the circus."

Norman was so excited, he made Vera excited, too.
"Let's run all the way home!" he shouted.

When they came to Norman's house, Vera said good-bye and hurried next door to her own home.

A big smile filled her face.

Vera rushed inside.

Her mother was in the bathroom. Baby Ruthie had unrolled all the toilet paper, stuffed it into the bowl, and flushed the toilet. There was water and toilet paper everywhere.

"Mom," Vera said loudly. "The teacher gave us our report cards today. Mine is full of A's!"

"That's good," Mother said. "I'm glad you're doing so well in school. I'll look at your report card later."

Vera went into the kitchen. Elaine and June were eating peanut butter and jelly sandwiches.

"Hi, Vera. I'll make you a sandwich," June offered.

"We got our report cards today," Vera said. "Mine is full of A's."

"Big deal," Elaine said. "Everyone gets A's in first grade."

"Right," June agreed.

Vera was not feeling so excited anymore. She quietly ate her sandwich.
Then she went to find her father.

Vera's father was in the bathroom. Lots of books and tools were
spread out on the floor. The toilet was in pieces.

"LOOK, DAD! I have all A's!"

"That's nice, Vera. I'm happy you're doing well in school.
I'll have to look at your report card later."

Vera went to her room and sat on her bed. Everyone is too busy to look at my report card, she thought.

Then she remembered what Norman had said. Norman's mother would probably jump up and down and hug him if he had a report card like Vera's.

She would make a special dinner and
take him to the circus.

Maybe she would even buy him the beautiful red scooter in the hardware store
at the shopping center.

Vera started to feel sad—sad and a little angry.

Maybe I should run away and look for a better family, like Norman's, Vera thought. My family doesn't have time for me. They probably won't even notice I'm gone.

Vera packed extra socks and underpants in a big red handkerchief. She took her rainbow-colored umbrella, in case it rained, and her bunny to keep her company at night. She took her report card, too, so she could show it to her new family.

There were woods near Vera's house.

Once she found her secret place, Vera sat down on the huge silvery tree branch next to the creek. Maybe the woods could be her new home, and she wouldn't bother at all with a family.

Vera made a wobbly house out of sticks and leaves, with a cozy grass nest inside. She would be a forest child.

After a while, Vera began to feel hungry. She could tell it was dinner time by the way the sun looked in the sky. Vera wondered if her family was missing her now.

She carefully wrapped up her things and left her secret place.

On her way home, Vera walked past Norman's house. She could smell his dinner cooking. Vera wished she could be Norman.

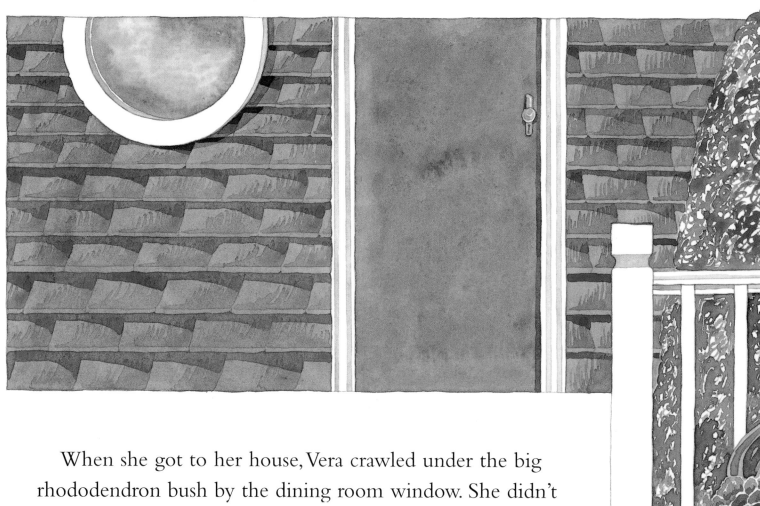

When she got to her house, Vera crawled under the big
rhododendron bush by the dining room window. She didn't
smell any dinner cooking. It was very quiet.

Maybe her family had moved away while she was gone.
Vera felt lonely.

Suddenly, the rhododendron branches rustled and moved apart.
"Here she is!" Elaine yelled, as she crawled under the big bush.

"Vera, where have you been? Everyone's been looking for you!"

"Really?" Vera asked.

Then June squeezed under the bush, too. "Vera," she said. "We've been riding our bikes all over. Mom went to the school and Dad is at the police station!"

The three girls crawled out from under the rhododendron bush.
Then Elaine rode her bike to the school and June rode to the police
station. Vera sat down on the front step of her quiet house to wait.

When everyone came home, Vera burst out, "I ran away because no one cared about my good report card!" Then she told them what Norman said about the special dinner and the circus.

"Oh, Vera," her mother said. "We're so sorry we didn't pay enough attention to your wonderful report card. But when you do well, you are doing well for yourself."

Vera looked at everyone. She knew her mother was right.

"Well," Vera said. "I guess
I will stay in this family.
But I am very HUNGRY!"

"Me, too," Elaine said. "And
there is no dinner to eat."

"We'll just have to go out
for pizza," sighed Mother.

Vera ate two big slices of pizza. It was fun being a forest child,
but her family had missed her. She had missed them, too.